Thomas' Day Off

Based on a story by **Craig Carlisle**

Adapted by **Fiona Munro**

First published in Great Britain 2023 by DEAN, part of Farshore
An imprint of HarperCollins*Publishers*
1 London Bridge Street, London SE1 9GF
www.farshore.co.uk

HarperCollins*Publishers*
Macken House, 39/40 Mayor Street Upper,
Dublin 1, D01 C9W8, Ireland

Based on a story by Craig Carlisle
Adapted by Fiona Munro

Based on the Railway Series by The Reverend W Awdry.
©2023 Gullane (Thomas) Limited.
Thomas the Tank Engine & Friends™ and Thomas & Friends™
are trademarks of Gullane (Thomas) Limited.
©2023 HIT Entertainment Limited. HIT and the HIT logo are
trademarks of HITEntertainment Limited.

ISBN 978 0 00 861745 5
Printed in China
002

A CIP catalogue record for this title is available from the British Library.

FSC
www.fsc.org

MIX
Paper | Supporting
responsible forestry
FSC™ C007454

This book contains FSC™ certified paper and other controlled
sources to ensure responsible forest management.

For more information visit: www.harpercollins.co.uk/green

CREATED BY *Britt* ALLCROFT

At Knapford Station, the engines waited patiently to see what their jobs would be for today.

"Would anyone like to deliver the mail?" asked Gordon.

"I would!" said Percy. "**ME! PICK ME!**"

"Next we have a delivery for Brendam Docks," Gordon continued.

"I'll do it!" said Diesel, quick as a flash.

"And I'm heading out to Whiff's Recycle Plant," Gordon went on. "That's it for today."

"Wait, what about me?" Thomas protested.

"It looks like you've got the day off, Thomas," smiled Gordon.

Thomas had never had a day by himself,
to do whatever he wanted.

He hurried to the obstacle course in the
Maintenance Yard, splashed through the puddles,
charged through the tunnel and whooshed
around the Loop-the-Loop.

" ***WHOO-HOO!*** Did you
see that, Per ... cy?"
But then he remembered that
Percy was miles away, delivering
the mail.

"I guess the obstacle course is
more fun with friends ..."

As Thomas rolled along the tracks, he began to feel very sorry for himself. He wasn't really looking where he was going and suddenly ... **_CRASH!_**

"Oh, I'm sorry!" he called out. "I'm Thomas, by the way," he went on, pretending he had found a new friend ... and not just an empty boxcar that couldn't talk back.

"Oh, your name is Boxy? I should show you around. There's a lot to see on Sodor."

Thomas hooked up Boxy and off they went, on an adventure of their own.

Thomas began showing Boxy all the sights on the island.

"We're coming up to Whiff's Recycle Plant," he began. Boxy rolled a little and suddenly, oops, one of the big bins toppled over and an old beach ball rolled out.

It may only have been a beach ball, but to Thomas it was part of his BIG adventure.

"It's the Orb of Destiny!" he said. "We can be knights guarding the Royal Treasure."

The 'Orb of Destiny' was suddenly caught by the wind and blew away. Thomas and Boxy chased it across forests and fields until they roared onto the docks.

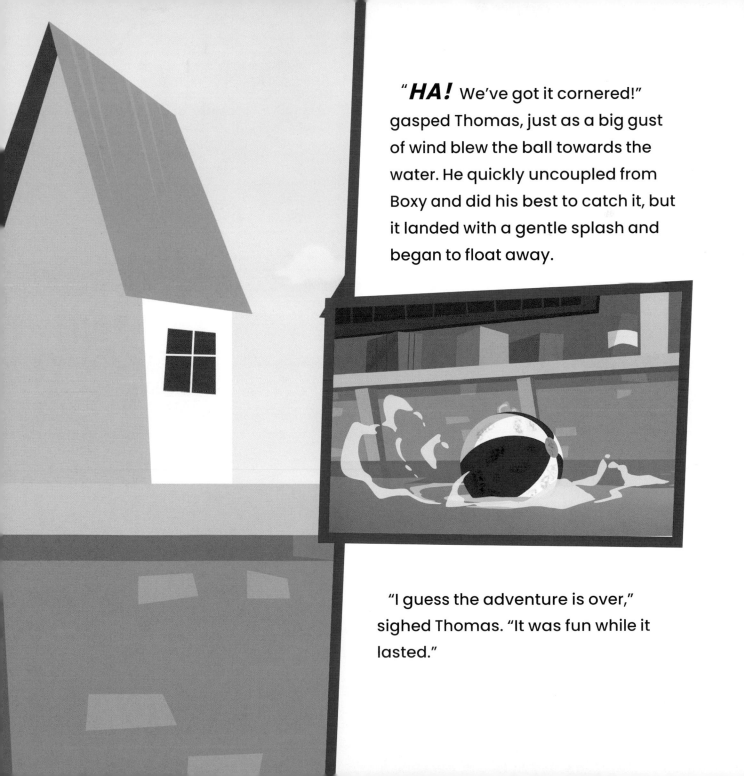

"**HA!** We've got it cornered!" gasped Thomas, just as a big gust of wind blew the ball towards the water. He quickly uncoupled from Boxy and did his best to catch it, but it landed with a gentle splash and began to float away.

"I guess the adventure is over," sighed Thomas. "It was fun while it lasted."

Just as Thomas was wondering where to take Boxy next, he heard a loud **CLANK**. Cranky had lifted Boxy onto Bulstrode the barge!

"Cranky! Wait!" Thomas said. "That boxcar isn't supposed to go out to sea."

Thomas watched anxiously as Boxy rolled from side to side.

"Or maybe he's exactly where he's supposed to be," he thought. "Great idea, Boxy! We can chase the Orb of Destiny by sea. Cranky can you lift me on board too?"

A few seconds later, the little engine was lowered onto the deck next to Boxy.

"Follow that Orb!" he called as loudly as he could.

Bulstrode was a little confused. "Orb?" he frowned. "All I can see is an old beach ball."

"That's no beach ball," said Thomas dramatically. "**THAT** is the Orb of Destiny!"

"Oooh, I love a good adventure. Let's get that Orb!" said Bulstrode.

But the sea was too rough. "Sorry, Thomas!"
said Bulstrode over the whooshing of the wind
and the sloshing of the waves.

As Bulstrode turned back towards calmer waters near the shore,
the big barge saw something whirling in the air above the deck.

"Ahoy, Thomas! The Orb of Destiny is heading for land!"

A few minutes later, Thomas and Boxy were safely off the barge and rolling along the tracks by the water's edge.

The Orb of Destiny was right in front of them.
This was their chance to catch it!

Just then, Diesel arrived. "Hey, Thomas," said Diesel. "What are you doing out here?"

"We have to catch the Orb of Destiny," Thomas replied, whizzing past.

Diesel was very confused. "Wait, you have to get the ..."

"... what?"

Thomas and Boxy clattered on down the tracks until **WHOOSH!** A sudden gust whisked the Orb up into a tree.

"Well," sighed Thomas. "The Orb of Destiny finally outsmarted us and got away."

He let out a long steamy sigh that puffed up into the tree.

The Orb jiggled in the leaves. Thomas puffed again and the Orb moved a little bit more ... and a little bit more ... until it slipped between the branches.

"Coming your way, Sir Boxy," said Thomas as the Orb bounced towards Boxy's open door, and the door clanged shut.

"Teamwork!" said Thomas. "Good job, Boxy."

"Has anyone seen Thomas?" asked Percy when he and the other engines got back to Tidmouth Sheds.

"I saw him earlier," said Diesel. "I think he said something about a 'Blob of Definitely'."

"It's an Orb of Destiny!" called Thomas, rattling down the tracks towards his friends.

"Cool," said Percy, a little confused. "How was your day off? Was it lonely being all by yourself?"

"No ..." began Thomas. "Boxy and I pretended to be knights guarding the Royal Treasure. Show them, Boxy."

All eyes were on Boxy as his side-door cranked open.

"You did all that for a beach ball?" asked Percy.

"No, silly!" laughed Thomas. "It's not a beach ball. It's the Orb of Destiny!"

"The beach ball ... I mean, the Orb of Destiny," cried out Diesel suddenly, "is flying away!"

"After it!" giggled Thomas, heading off down the track in a cloud of steam, with his friends close behind.

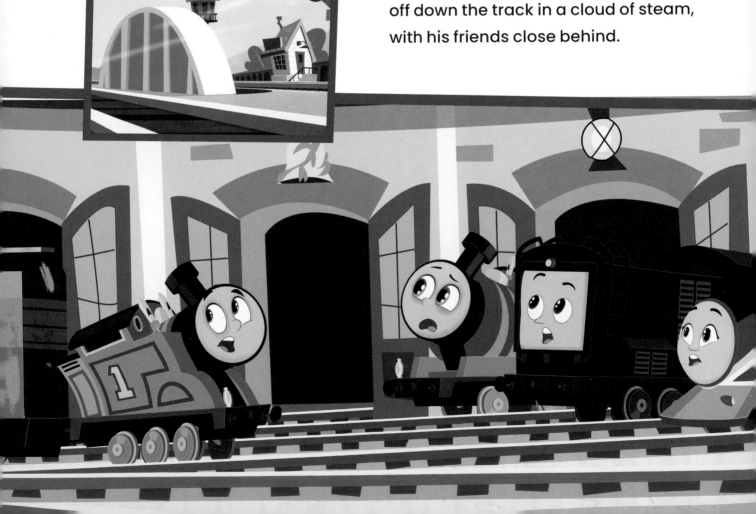